UNICORN ACADEMY

Moonbeam closed her eyes and started to sway. "The earth is shaking," she said dreamily. "Rocks are falling from the sky. Zara!" Moonbeam's eyes snapped open. Her nostrils flared, and she was trembling. She stared at Zara with wide eyes. "I saw you in danger," she said.

LOOK OUT FOR MORE
ADVENTURES WITH

UNICORN ★ ACADEMY

NATURE MAGIC

Lily and Feather
Phoebe and Shimmer
Zara and Moonbeam
Aisha and Silver

★ ★ ★

UNICORN ACADEMY

NATURE MAGIC 3

Zara and
Moonbeam

JULIE SYKES
illustrated by LUCY TRUMAN

A STEPPING STONE BOOK™
Random House 🏠 New York

Text copyright © 2020 by Julie Sykes and Linda Chapman
Cover art and interior illustrations copyright © 2020 by Lucy Truman

All rights reserved. Published in the United States by Random House
Children's Books, a division of Penguin Random House LLC, New York.
Originally published in paperback in the United Kingdom by
Nosy Crow Ltd, London, in 2020.

Random House and the colophon are registered trademarks and A Stepping
Stone Book and the colophon are trademarks of Penguin Random House LLC.

Visit us on the Web! rhcbooks.com

Educators and librarians, for a variety of teaching tools, visit us at
RHTeachersLibrarians.com

Library of Congress Cataloging-in-Publication Data is available upon request.
ISBN 978-0-593-42675-3 (trade) — ISBN 978-0-593-42676-0 (lib. bdg.) —
ISBN 978-0-593-42677-7 (ebook)

Printed in the United States of America
10 9 8 7 6 5 4 3 2
First American Edition

For Khadijah and her magical mum,
Rumena Aktar

CHAPTER 1

"We won!" Zara clapped as her unicorn, Moonbeam, galloped across the dry grass and splashed into Sparkle Lake.

"Yay!" Moonbeam kicked up her hooves, showering them both with the glittering water.

Zara pushed her straight brown hair away from her face. "Hurry up, slowpokes!" she called to her friends. "It's nice and cool!"

With whoops of delight, Phoebe, Lily, and Aisha followed on their unicorns Shimmer, Feather, and Silver.

"It was so hot and stuffy this morning in class,

I honestly thought I was going to die. I think we should ask Ms. Rosemary if we can have afternoon lessons in the lake," said Phoebe, pushing her long blond braids over her shoulders. "It would be awesome!"

Zara laughed. "Yep, because she'll *definitely* agree to that!"

It was summer and Unicorn Island was in the middle of a heat wave. At first, Zara and her friends in Amethyst dorm had loved the long hot days and nights. But after several weeks of high temperatures, the heat was becoming unbearable. The grass had turned to a yellow crisp, and the flowers and plants had all wilted. The fountain was drier and the lake had shrunk, leaving a rim of cracked, dried mud around the edge.

The unicorns splashed and kicked water at each other with their hooves.

Lily leaned forward and whispered in Feather's

ear. Suddenly the lake began to ripple. Zara smelled the sweet, sugary scent of magic and saw sparkles bubbling up through the water from Feather's hooves. The ripples grew stronger until the water rose in a tall, glittering wave. It arced high over Zara, Phoebe, and Aisha. Zara held her breath, expecting to get soaked.

CRACK! More magical sparkles fizzed in the air and the wave exploded, raining shimmering droplets down on everyone.

Zara laughed, enjoying the cool mist falling on her face and hair.

Lily, Phoebe, and Aisha clapped and cheered. "Go, Feather and Shimmer!"

Zara clapped too, but she couldn't help feeling a little bit envious. She knew Lily's unicorn, Feather, had created the wave with her special moving magic. And then Phoebe's unicorn, Shimmer, had broken it with his energy magic. When would

Moonbeam discover her magic? The unicorns usually found their special magical powers during their first year at the academy. Those who didn't had to stay for a second year with their partners.

"He's coming back," Moonbeam whispered.

Zara leaned over her unicorn's neck. "Who's coming back?" she asked.

"He is," said Moonbeam dreamily.

"But who?" said Zara. "Who are you talking about?" She felt a prickle of frustration. Moonbeam often went off into daydreams. "What do you mean, Moonbeam?"

Moonbeam jumped in surprise as if she was waking up. "Oh, sorry! I'm not sure what I was saying."

"Hurry up, you two!" Lily called from the bank. "Lunchtime's nearly over, and we need to dry off before afternoon classes start."

"Okay," Zara called. "We're coming!"

But Moonbeam didn't move. "Zara, wait, I feel strange, like there's magic all around me. My skin's tingling."

Zara shrugged. "Shimmer and Feather were just doing magic. That must be what you can sense."

"This is different," Moonbeam insisted. "For a moment back there I . . . I felt like I'd found my own magic."

Zara frowned. "But you didn't do anything magical, Moonbeam."

"No, but I had a feeling," said Moonbeam.

Zara sighed. Moonbeam was always going on about feelings and how important they were. "Moonbeam, you know I want you to find your magic just as much as you do, but imagining it isn't going to help. Come on, let's go dry off.

We have Care of Unicorns after lunch, and Ms. Rosemary hates it when students are late."

For a moment, she thought Moonbeam was going to argue, but then she splashed out of the lake. As they reached the bank, Zara slid from Moonbeam's back and ran over to join her friends.

"That was a fun water fight!" she said, flopping down on the grass next to Phoebe.

Aisha giggled and tightened her high ponytail. "I thought Feather was going to cover us with that wave!"

Phoebe grinned. "It wasn't half as scary as the enormous tidal wave that almost hit us when we camped on the cliff, though."

Lily nodded. "I will never, ever forget that. It was terrifying! We were so lucky that Shimmer was able to save us using his energy magic."

Back in the spring, a huge tidal wave had nearly

destroyed a part of the coast that the girls had been camping on. They'd only escaped thanks to Shimmer's magic powers. He had used his ability to throw balls of magic energy to break up the wave before it could ruin anything.

That wasn't the only environmental problem that had happened this year. Just after they had started at Unicorn Academy, purple tornadoes had swept through the island. One had almost destroyed the academy, but Feather had used her moving magic to send it safely out to sea.

Zara suddenly had a worrying thought. "What if this heat wave is being caused by the same person who caused the tornadoes and the tidal wave?"

Phoebe sat up. "You mean it could be part of someone's evil plan?"

"It's a possibility," said Zara.

"If it is part of someone's plan, we need to be careful," said Lily.

Phoebe waved her hands dramatically. "We could be attacked at any moment!"

"Don't exaggerate, Phoebe," Zara said with a grin. She really liked Phoebe, but she did turn every little thing into something more dramatic.

"But what if this evil person is planning to use this heat wave to hurt us—and our unicorns?" Phoebe exclaimed.

"We need to find out who's causing these things before it gets worse," said Zara. "We know it's a man because we heard a man's voice in the tornado and tidal wave saying he wouldn't be stopped. And before the tsunami struck, we heard that a cloaked man had been hanging around the village where the wave was heading."

"None of those things tells us who the person

is, though," Lily pointed out. "Or why he's trying to harm the island."

"True." A look of determination crossed Zara's eyes. "I vote we try to find him and stop him for good." She glanced around at her three friends. "Who's with me? Who wants to solve this mystery?"

"Me!" cried Phoebe, Lily, and Aisha as their unicorns whinnied and stamped their hooves.

CHAPTER 2

The girls excitedly discussed ideas for how to track down the evil man as they rode back to the stables at the end of lunchtime.

"Zara," Moonbeam said as she and Zara reached her stable. "Can I talk to you? It's about these feelings I keep having."

Zara wanted to talk about the mystery instead, but she forced herself to smile. "Of course."

"I might be wrong," said Moonbeam. "But I keep seeing pictures in my head, and when I do, I start to say strange stuff out loud. Do you think it could be my magic?"

"Your magic? But, Moonbeam, the stuff you say, well, it's just . . ." Zara caught herself. She'd been about to say *silly.* "It just doesn't seem to mean anything," she finished.

Moonbeam frowned. "But what if it *does* mean something? What if it's important?"

Zara stroked her. She really wanted Moonbeam to find her magic, but seeing pictures in her head

and saying strange things didn't sound like magic to her. "I really don't think it has anything to do with your magic powers," she said. "But I'm sure you'll find them soon," she added quickly.

Ms. Rosemary was waiting for them in the stables, wearing a big floppy hat and sunglasses.

"Good afternoon," she said when the students arrived. "Today we are learning how to keep our unicorns cool in hot weather. Can anyone think of a way?"

Spike from Topaz dorm put his hand up. "Make them wear sunglasses and a big hat, just like yours, Ms. R!"

Everyone burst out laughing, and Ms. Rosemary smiled. "That's an interesting idea, Spike. I'll think about it," she said. "Any other suggestions?"

A familiar sharp voice cut across the stables.

"Heatstroke is a serious matter, Ms. Rosemary. Rather than making jokes, don't you think you

should be teaching the students about what to do in the current weather conditions?"

Zara's heart sank as Mr. Long, the school inspector, walked through the stables' doors. Ms. Tulip, the Riding teacher, was hurrying along behind him. Why was he back? He'd inspected the academy only a few months ago.

"Not him again," groaned Phoebe.

Moonbeam gasped. "Zara!" she hissed. "I was right! I said someone was coming back, didn't I?"

Zara patted her. "It's just a coincidence, Moonbeam. You can't really think you predicted that Mr. Long would come back today. You're letting your imagination run away with you."

Moonbeam hung her head. "Maybe," she muttered.

"I wonder why he's here," whispered Lily. Ms. Rosemary was clearly wondering the same thing.

"Good afternoon, Mr. Long," she said. "What

brings you back to the academy so soon? I thought your inspection was complete."

Mr. Long mopped his forehead with a handkerchief. "I inspected the school, but I didn't have a chance to inspect the stables or the quality of riding lessons."

Ms. Tulip stepped forward. "As part of the inspector's visit—and so he can experience the teaching himself—I have offered to teach him to ride." She tucked a dark curl of hair behind her ear and blushed. "Mr. Long, would you like to meet Rocket, my unicorn?" she asked.

"Indeed I would," Mr. Long said.

"Then, please—follow me."

"Urgh!" whispered Phoebe as Ms. Tulip led Mr. Long to Rocket's stable.

"Poor Ms. Tulip!" said Zara. "I can't think of anything worse than teaching bossy Mr. Long."

"Did you see how nice she was being? She must

be hoping he gives her a good report." Phoebe fluttered her hands and fluffed up her hair. Imitating Ms. Tulip, she said, "Oh, let me teach you, Mr. Long!"

Lily rushed to Ms. Tulip's defense. "Don't be mean. Mr. Long had better give Ms. Tulip's teaching a good report, or I'll . . . I'll complain about *him*!"

Aisha nodded. "I don't understand why he's back. He spent lots of time watching our riding lessons with Ms. Tulip when he was here before. Why does he need to see more?"

"I hope he falls off Rocket," grumbled Phoebe. She clapped a hand over her mouth. "Actually, I didn't mean that. I hope he learns to ride superfast, gives Ms. Tulip a great report, and then goes away again really quickly!"

"Me too," said Lily. "It's bad enough having

to deal with a heat wave
without having to put
up with Mr. Long too!"

Her words sent a
thought exploding
into Zara's mind.
She gasped.

"What? What is it?"
demanded Lily.

But before Zara
could speak, Ms.
Rosemary clapped
her hands together

for silence. "All right. Pay attention, please. This
afternoon we are going to make a sunscreen to
protect your unicorn's nose. The ingredients are
laid out in the storeroom. Go collect everything,
and read through the instructions."

While the rest of the class headed for the storeroom, Zara pulled her friends into a huddle.

"What's going on?" said Phoebe eagerly. "You look like a snot-nosed flapdoodle just sneezed on you!"

"It's Mr. Long!" hissed Zara. "Maybe he's the person causing all the problems! We know he studied geology at college. What if he's responsible for all the weather problems we've had this year? He was with us when the tidal wave struck, and he's here now, when the heat wave is getting really bad." She gazed at her friends. "Maybe the extreme weather we've had this year has been caused by him!"

CHAPTER 3

"Girls! What are you doing?" Ms. Rosemary called across the stables. "I told you to get your ingredients and instructions."

"Sorry, Ms. Rosemary!" said Zara quickly. "We'll talk about this later," she hissed to the others as they jogged to the storeroom.

All through the lesson, Zara's mind raced. Could Mr. Long really be the mystery man? The more she thought about it, the more everything seemed to fit together. *But there has to be proof*, she reminded herself firmly.

She was so busy thinking about it that she
added too much honey powder to her sunscreen.
She only realized when Moonbeam couldn't stop

sneezing after she tried to lick the sunscreen off her nose because it tasted so good!

As soon as the lesson was over, the girls raced up to their dorm, where they could talk in private. Amethyst dorm had four beds set around the room, each with a lavender-colored bedspread. There was a fluffy purple rug on the floor, and they sat in a circle on top of it.

"It's him! You're right, Zara. I'm sure of it!" exclaimed Phoebe. "Mr. Long is so horrible. He's really bossy and a complete show-off!"

"We have to tell the teachers," said Lily.

"No," said Zara quickly. "We don't have any proof, although the evidence does seem to point to him. Listen." She pulled a mini notebook from her pocket, where she had scribbled some notes. "Number one: Mr. Long is very smart. He's written all sorts of scientific articles. He might know a way to make bad weather happen."

"Or he could be working with someone who does," said Phoebe excitedly. "He doesn't have a unicorn himself, but he may know someone who has a unicorn that can do weather magic."

"Good point," said Zara.

"What else do you have on your list?" asked Lily.

"Number two: The first time Mr. Long arrived at the academy, a dormant volcano near the school began to wake up. Activity from that volcano caused the tidal wave, so maybe he did something to the volcano on his way here.

"Number three: It was his idea to go camping on the west coast of the island, where we were almost drowned by the tidal wave." Zara paused to look around at her friends. "He wanted us to go there!"

Phoebe pretended to be the inspector. *"Volcanoes are a particular interest of mine."* Her eyes glimmered with excitement exactly like Mr. Long's did when he was showing off.

"But why would Mr. Long want to cause such bad things to happen to the island?" said Aisha.

"Well," said Zara. "I looked Mr. Long up when he was here last time. Apparently he wanted to work as a researcher, but nobody wanted his research. That's how he ended up as a school inspector. Maybe he wants to get back at the island because he's upset."

Phoebe's eyes widened. "Or . . . or . . . ," she spluttered in her excitement, "maybe he thinks that if enough bad weather happens, then people will pay him to do research and he'll be able to stop being an inspector!"

"Great idea, Phoebe!" said Zara excitedly, writing it down.

"What about the other clues we had—the cloaked stranger who was seen by the deserted cottage, and the button we found there," said Lily. "The stranger couldn't have been Mr. Long. He was at the academy with us when the villagers say they spotted him."

"That's true," said Zara slowly. "Maybe the stranger at the cottage is completely unrelated to the tidal wave. It could be a red herring—that's what false clues are called."

"What about the button?" asked Aisha.

Zara jumped to her feet and got the button from her nightstand. "This could be a red herring too," she said, turning the pale gray button over in her fingers. It had a mark on it that looked like a two-headed serpent twisted around a strange symbol.

"Or it could have been dropped by Mr. Long at some point when we were there," said Phoebe as Zara put the button down so they could all

see it. "He could have gone to the cottage when we were getting our campsites ready. Maybe he did something there that caused the tidal wave to hit."

"If you look at the mark, it almost looks like a letter in really curly writing," said Aisha, tracing the pattern with one finger.

"It's an L!" said Lily with a gasp. "Look, everyone! L for *Long*!"

"I knew it!" exclaimed Phoebe. "He *is* the evil villain!"

"We don't know for sure that it's his, or that he's responsible for the weather problems," said Zara quickly. "We need to find evidence."

"How do we do that?" asked Phoebe.

Zara grinned. "We spy on him, of course!"

Phoebe squealed in delight. "Oh yes, let's do that! We'll prove he's to blame!"

Zara's eyes shone. "And if he is, we'll stop him, no matter what!"

★

After dinner that evening, there was a quiz. It was held outside, where it was cooler. Zara, Phoebe, Lily, and Aisha carried some blankets and spread them under an apple tree. When everyone was there, Ms. Nettles handed out paper and a pencil to each group.

"Ready?" she asked, smiling at the students. "Then the first question is, which rare species of beetle lives in the crater of a volcano?"

"The fire beetle," Zara whispered to the others.

Everyone stared at her. "How do you know that?" hissed Phoebe.

Zara grinned. "You know science is my thing. I read up on volcanoes when Mount Inferno suddenly became active again."

The quiz questions covered everything—taking care of unicorns, geology, famous scientists, wild animals, and general knowledge. Zara talked to her group in whispers before she wrote down each answer. Meanwhile, Topaz dorm talked loudly nearby, and seemed to be competing to come up with the silliest answers.

"How long are the legs of the very rare, gold-striped, pygmy unicorn?" asked Ms. Nettles.

"Long enough to reach the ground!" shouted Spike, earning a glare from Mr. Long as he arrived late with Ms. Tulip.

Mr. Long had a rug tucked under his arm, and Ms. Tulip was carrying a jug of iced blackcurrant juice and two glasses on a tray. Ms. Tulip poured Mr. Long a drink as he spread the rug on the ground. "She really is trying her hardest to get a good report!" whispered Phoebe.

Ms. Nettles waited for them to sit down before continuing. "Who was the first person to successfully combine science with magic?"

"Count Lysander Thornberry," Mr. Long said immediately. "He used science to amplify magic to make a rain machine. I went to school with him. He could have been an amazing research scientist. But he got mad when a few academic papers questioned whether his weather machines were needed, when we have unicorns who have weather magic. He left college, returning to his family castle to continue his work there."

Ms. Nettles blinked. "Thank you for answering

29

the question so fully, Mr. Long, but the quiz is for the students."

Mr. Long raised his eyebrows. "I really believe you need harder questions, Ms. Nettles. Perhaps you will allow me to ask a question. What did Count Thornberry call his rain machine?"

"The Big Drip!" hissed Spike in a loud whisper.

Everyone started to giggle, but Mr. Long silenced them with a glare. "The *Pluviam Machina*. Really, Ms. Nettles, I am surprised that the students are so lacking in scientific knowledge. Perhaps I should run some classes to teach you about the incredible scientists from our island."

"I would sign up for those!" Ms. Tulip said eagerly.

"Ooh, me too!" whispered Phoebe, imitating Ms. Tulip's goofy expression.

"Stop it!" Zara giggled. "You'll get us into trouble."

Ms. Nettles pursed her lips. "Thank you, Mr. Long. Now, if I may continue with our quiz?"

The quiz ran over time, thanks to Mr. Long's interruptions. The girls of Amethyst dorm cheered loudly when Ms. Nettles announced them as the winners. She handed them a massive bag of candy. "Don't eat your prize all at once," she said.

Mr. Long sniffed. "Educational books would have been a better prize." He pulled out his handkerchief and dabbed at his brow. Even outside, it was very hot.

"Everyone, please check on your unicorns and then off to bed!" said Ms. Nettles, ignoring him.

Mr. Long offered his hand to help Ms. Tulip up. "Will you join me at the stables and talk

me through the students' evening routine, Ms. Tulip?"

"Of course," she said.

Zara watched them head toward the stables. *Be very careful, Mr. Long*, she thought. *We're on to you, so you'd better watch out!*

CHAPTER 4

The next day, Amethyst dorm used their free time to spy on Mr. Long. The remote-controlled trolleys that moved bales of straw around the stables were useful for cover. The girls hid behind them and watched him following Ms. Tulip around, clipboard in hand. Then they watched him take a riding lesson in the arena with Ms. Tulip and her unicorn, Rocket.

It was fun spying on Mr. Long, but they didn't see him do anything suspicious. *Not that he would do anything when he's with Ms. Tulip*, Zara thought as she headed back to Amethyst dorm after dinner. *We*

need to spy on him when he's on his own, maybe sneak into
his room . . .

Her thoughts were interrupted by the sight of Mr. Long crossing the hallway ahead of her and climbing a spiral staircase that led up one of the towers. Zara frowned. *Why is he going upstairs?* There were only two rooms up that staircase— Diamond dorm on the first floor and a storeroom at the very top.

Zara ran after Mr. Long. Between the two floors, she heard Mr. Long's footsteps stop. She paused, hovering outside the door to Diamond dorm. If he came back, she'd have to pretend she was just going to visit one of the girls there. She listened hard and heard a door open.

Zara waited. What was Mr. Long doing? She crept on up the stairs to find a large wooden cupboard in the wall. Zara pushed at the door gently, her heart thudding. What would she do if Mr. Long was inside? But to her relief, she saw that it just had a stack of old packing crates and some cardboard boxes.

Zara continued up to the top floor, but to her surprise, there was no sign of Mr. Long there, either. Where had he gone? She stepped inside the storeroom, picking her way between the students' suitcases, shelves of empty potion bottles, and some old paintings to the window. It was covered in dust.

Feeling very puzzled, Zara went downstairs. This didn't make sense. Mr. Long had definitely gone up the stairs. So where was he now? She

wanted to talk to the others, but her dorm was empty. Glancing at the clock, she realized it was getting late and her friends must be getting their unicorns ready for the night. Zara felt a pang of guilt. Moonbeam would be wondering where she was. She hurried outside, running across the dry grass to the stables.

Moonbeam whickered happily when she saw her. "There you are!" she said. "I was worried that I'd done something to upset you."

"Of course not!" Zara laid her head against Moonbeam's neck. "I'm sorry I was late. Something really weird happened, Moonbeam . . . Moonbeam?" She felt a pang of worry as she saw that Moonbeam's eyelids had closed and she was swaying slightly.

"I see a cloaked man," Moonbeam whispered. "And a dark green book."

Zara put a hand on her unicorn's side to steady her. "Are you feeling okay?"

Moonbeam's eyes stayed closed. "A red desert that stretches on and rocks falling from the sky," she continued. "Danger comes."

Zara frowned. "Moonbeam! What's happening to you? Is it the heat? Do you want a drink?" It was very warm in the stables, even with the new fans Ms. Tulip had installed.

Moonbeam's eyes flew open. "What just happened?"

"I don't know," said Zara. "You were saying stuff about a cloaked man and a book, a desert and rocks."

"I was seeing pictures in my head again, Zara. Clearer this time." Excitement lit up Moonbeam's dark eyes. "I think I've started to see things that are going to happen. Yesterday, I had a vision about a man arriving at the school and then, just after that, Mr. Long appeared. This morning, I had a vision that Ms. Tulip would give him a riding lesson in the arena, and she did. I . . . I think I might have seer magic—magic that lets me look into the future!"

Moonbeam sounded so hopeful that Zara didn't want to disappoint her, but it didn't seem very likely. "Moonbeam, if this was your magic, there would be sparks. And you should be able to smell burnt sugar, shouldn't you? That's what happens when the other unicorns use their powers."

"My magic's different," said Moonbeam. "I feel it inside me. It's like having sparks in my head."

"That doesn't sound like magic to me," said Zara.

Moonbeam stamped a hoof in frustration. "So why do I keep seeing the same pictures over and over again? A cloaked man who makes me feel scared, a desert, a damaged green book, and rocks falling." She glanced at Zara. "How do you explain that?"

Zara hesitated. "I . . . I don't know. But I'm sure there *is* a logical explanation, and I don't think it's because of magic." Moonbeam's face fell. Zara felt bad. She hated upsetting her, but she knew it was wrong to lie to her unicorn. "I love you, Moonbeam," she went on awkwardly. "You know that. You're a dreamer and I'm scientific, so there are bound to be things we disagree on. But that doesn't mean that we can't be really good partners and best friends."

"I guess," sighed Moonbeam. She gave her an anxious look. "But, Zara, promise me you'll be careful when you're spying on Mr. Long. If he is the cloaked figure I've been seeing in my visions, then I don't trust him at all."

Zara hugged her. "That's something we do agree on!" she said with a smile.

CHAPTER 5

Zara waited until she and her friends were all back in the dorm before calling a meeting. She told them how she'd followed Mr. Long up the tower and how he had vanished into thin air.

Phoebe's eyes widened. "Maybe Mr. Long can use magic to disappear?"

Zara frowned. "But how? He doesn't have a unicorn, and I don't think there's any other magic that can make you vanish. We must keep spying!"

★

The following day at lunch, Ms. Nettles announced that afternoon lessons were canceled because

41

there was an important staff meeting.

"Let's go sneak into Mr. Long's room during the meeting," said Zara.

The others agreed. They waited until all the adults were together, and then they hurried to his room. They tried the door, but it was locked.

Zara groaned in frustration. She felt sure that if she could search Mr. Long's room, she would find a clue that would prove he was the one responsible for the bad weather.

"Never mind," said Lily. "It's too hot inside. Let's take the unicorns to the meadow. We can all swim in the stream."

"Not that there's much stream left." Aisha sighed. "I really hope this heat wave goes away soon. All the streams and rivers are starting to dry up."

They exchanged anxious looks. The water from Sparkle Lake was magical. Unicorns needed to drink the water in order for their magic to stay

strong. It flowed away from the lake around the island in rivers and streams, where it nourished crops, people, and animals. If the water dried up, then the unicorns would lose their magic powers and all of Unicorn Island would suffer.

The girls headed to the stables.

"I had another vision!" Moonbeam told Zara excitedly when Zara entered her stall. "It happened just now. I saw a dark tunnel. It felt dangerous."

Zara patted her. "Okay, well, we'll watch out for dangerous, dark tunnels and avoid them," she said, failing to hide her grin.

Moonbeam stamped a front hoof. "Don't laugh at me! I'm not making these things up, Zara!"

"Sorry!" Zara said. But it was clear Moonbeam felt hurt. She refused to join Zara in the stream when everyone swam, even when it ended in a huge water fight. Zara tried being extra nice to

her, but nothing she said could get Moonbeam to join them in the water.

As the sun started to sink in the sky, they headed back to the stables to get the unicorns some sky berries before going in for their own dinner. Sky berries were the unicorns' favorite food. They were full of the vitamins they needed to stay healthy and keep their magic strong. As they passed the barn next to the stables, Zara noticed the big doors were open. Hearing a noise, she peeked in and gasped as she saw a tall, thin figure duck behind some hay bales at the far end.

"Come on, Zara, I'm starving!" called Aisha.

Putting her finger to her lips, Zara quickly beckoned her friends over. She pointed to the bales of hay. "Someone's there," she mouthed. "I think it's Mr. Long!"

She heard a rustle behind the bales and a soft click.

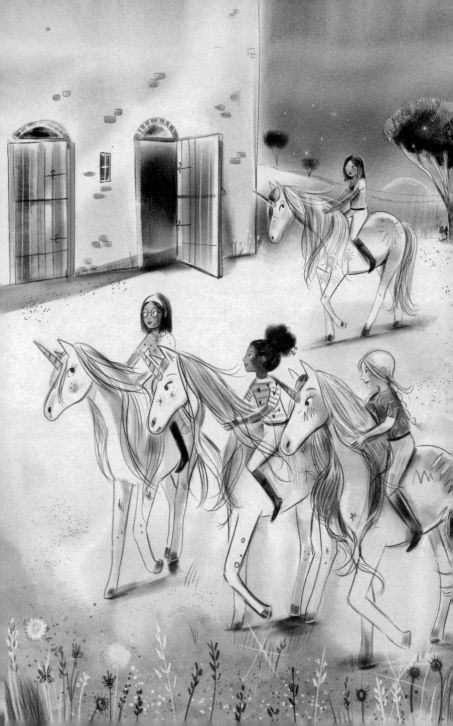

Zara ran up to the wall of bales. "Got you!" she shouted. She stopped in surprise as she looked over the top of them. "There's no one here!" she exclaimed.

Phoebe burst out laughing. "You're seeing things, Zara."

"I'm not!" she exclaimed. "I'm sure I saw Mr. Long!" Her friends looked at her in disbelief.

Zara flushed, suddenly realizing how Moonbeam must have felt when she didn't believe her. "There *was* someone here."

"Okay, but where?" Lily joined her and searched the barn. Suddenly she gasped and pointed to the floor. "What's that?" Crouching down, she showed Zara a big ring in the floor that had been hidden under the loose hay.

Zara brushed the hay away with her hands. The others crowded around.

"It's the handle of a trap door!" Zara heaved it open and it fell back with a heavy thud.

"It's a secret passage," breathed Phoebe.

"Oh wow! My mom told me the school has lots of secret passages and tunnels," said Lily. "She and her friends found some when they were here. Maybe this is one of them."

"Let's investigate," said Zara eagerly. "The person I saw just now must have escaped down it. Let's find out where it goes."

"Zara, wait!" Moonbeam stepped forward. "I'm sure this is the dark, dangerous tunnel from my vision."

"Vision?" echoed Phoebe, looking at Moonbeam. "What are you talking about?"

"It's nothing," Zara said quickly. She didn't want her friends and their unicorns all laughing at Moonbeam. "Just Moonbeam daydreaming as usual. You know what she's like!" She saw a hurt expression cross Moonbeam's face and felt bad. But she was sure that if Moonbeam said she could see into the future, everyone would tease her.

"Come on," Zara urged. "Let's see where this goes." She looked around at her friends before stepping down into the darkness.

CHAPTER 6

Phoebe, Lily, and Aisha followed Zara into the tunnel. Zara was good at climbing and guided the others, carefully feeling for handholds and footholds in the cold stone wall.

"Be careful!" whinnied the unicorns as they waited at the top.

"Very, very careful," added Moonbeam.

Once all the girls had climbed down, they set off. Zara traced her hand along the rough stone wall as she edged forward, her eyes gradually getting used to the darkness. She could hear the steady drip of water.

"Eeek!" squealed Phoebe, slipping on a stone.

"Shh!" Zara stopped, motioning for everyone to be quiet. What if Mr. Long was ahead of them and heard Phoebe? What if he came back and attacked?

They waited, but there was no sound. Carefully, they set off again. The sound of water began to get louder as they walked, until suddenly the tunnel opened into a chamber. Rainbow water trickled down the damp walls.

"I think we might be under Sparkle Lake." Zara squinted into the darkness and saw two more tunnels leading out of the chamber. "There are two ways out of here—" She gasped as she spotted something white lying on the floor at the entrance to one of the tunnels. "Look!" She hurried to pick it up. It was a white handkerchief. She could just make out the initials E.L. in one corner.

"This belongs to Mr. Long!" she exclaimed. "I saw him with it yesterday. He must have

dropped it. It's proof he's been down here. He *was* the person I saw going into the tunnel."

Phoebe grabbed her arm. "What should we do?"

Zara took a breath. What if Moonbeam really was having visions and her strange feelings were true? She'd said the tunnel was dangerous. But they couldn't give up now.

"Let's go on!" she said. The others nodded.

As Zara walked into the tunnel where the handkerchief had been lying, she was grateful that her friends were right behind her. The passageway began to climb upward, getting steeper and narrower. Finally it ended in a small space with a chimney rising up from it. Zara felt around the stones. Her hand caught against something round, and she accidentally pressed it. There was a creaking noise and a small door swung open.

Ducking through, Zara saw that the door led out into a fireplace in a round room.

"We're in one of the towers in the academy," she said, climbing out.

The others followed her.

"It's a secret room!" Aisha gasped, looking around.

There was an old wooden desk to one side, and the walls were lined with curved shelves with glass jars. Over the fireplace hung a picture of a beautiful unicorn with a long golden mane.

"I wonder what that thing does," said Zara, spotting a lever in the opposite wall and hurrying over. She pulled it and jumped back as the wall started to spin slowly like a revolving door. "This must be the way out!" she said in excitement. The wall revolved back into place. Zara pulled the lever again, and this time she and the others

slipped out as the wall turned. They found themselves in a cupboard full of empty cardboard boxes and wooden crates. "Maybe it's not the way out after all," said Aisha in surprise.

"Wait . . ." Zara looked around. "I think it's the cupboard above Diamond dorm." She spotted the door and turned the handle. It swung open, and she stepped out onto the stairs between Diamond dorm and the top floor of the tower.

"This is where I lost Mr. Long yesterday,"

she said excitedly. "So that's why he keeps disappearing. He's using secret tunnels to move around the school!"

"Do you think he heard us following him?" said Phoebe.

"What do you think he will do if he did?" asked Lily.

"Nothing," said Zara, sounding more confident than she felt. "I bet Mr. Long wouldn't want Ms. Nettles to know we found him sneaking around using the secret tunnels, so he won't do anything."

"Shouldn't we tell Ms. Nettles?" said Aisha.

Zara thought for a moment. "No. Sneaking around is strange, but we need proof that he's actually up to no good. We're on to him now. As soon as we find evidence, then we'll tell Ms. Nettles. Let's all be careful, though, okay?"

"Definitely!" said Phoebe. She gave a dramatic

shiver. "After all, we don't know what he's up to!"

They hurried back to the barn to tell their unicorns what had happened.

"I told you I saw a dangerous tunnel!" Moonbeam muttered to Zara as they walked back to the stables. "What if Mr. Long had attacked you? You shouldn't have gone down there."

Zara glanced at her. Moonbeam had been upset with her ever since she had returned. "We had to. If we hadn't gone down there, we wouldn't have found out that Mr. Long was using the tunnels to sneak around. And it wasn't that dangerous down there. Your feeling was wrong."

"I don't think it was," said Moonbeam. "It could have been dangerous." She gave Zara an unhappy look. "You embarrassed me in front of everyone back there in the barn, Zara, by saying I'm just daydreaming. I'm not. I'm having *magical visions*. You might not believe it, but I know it's true."

She tossed her mane and stomped into her stable. Zara sighed. She wished Moonbeam would stop going on about being able to see into the future. It just wasn't possible! She fetched Moonbeam a big bucket of sky berries, but Moonbeam stood at the back of her stable, refusing to look at her.

★

The girls went to their dorm to wash their hands before dinner. Entering the dining hall, Zara saw Mr. Long staring at them. She got the feeling that he'd seen her in the doorway to the barn and knew she and her friends had followed him. Zara lost her appetite, even though it was her favorite meal of lasagna followed by ice cream.

After dinner, Ms. Nettles clapped her hands for

silence. "The heat wave has gone on much longer than we expected. The island's rivers and streams are drying up. Mr. Long suggested investigating one of the nearby rivers to see what we can learn about the drought. I agree that it will be a good learning experience, so the whole school will be going on a field trip tomorrow. You can collect your camping equipment from the hall after breakfast. A teacher will be in charge of each dorm and will show you which part of the river to study." Peering down her nose at the students, Ms. Nettles shushed the burst of excited chatter with a stern look. "The groups are Ms. Rivers—Opal dorm; Ms. Rosemary—Topaz dorm; Ms. Tulip and Mr. Long—Amethyst dorm . . ."

No! Not him. Zara couldn't believe their bad luck. They were being sent away from the safety of the academy to a lonely riverside with Mr. Long! *Ms. Tulip will be with us too,* Zara reminded herself.

Surely she would protect them if he tried to harm them. *Unless he does something to harm Ms. Tulip,* she thought with a shiver.

She looked across at Mr. Long and saw him watching them.

Zara felt as if an ice cube was running down her spine. What if Moonbeam actually could see into the future? And what if Mr. Long was the mysterious, scary cloaked figure Moonbeam had been seeing? They could all be in serious danger!

CHAPTER 7

The following morning, Zara, Phoebe, Aisha, and Lily went straight to the hall.

"Here are our things," said Lily, seeing a pile of tents, rolled sleeping bags, and backpacks. "How come we seem to have more than everyone else?"

"Because your dorm will be going twice as far as everyone else." Mr. Long came up behind them, making them all jump. "Ms. Nettles seems to think your group is trustworthy enough to go farthest from the academy. I wanted to take enough food and water in case we get stuck there for some reason."

His words gave Zara goosebumps, but she made herself give him a cool look. She was with her friends, their unicorns, and Ms. Tulip. They were more than a match for him!

She turned her back on Mr. Long. "Are you ready, Phoebe? Give me a hand with our tent."

"How long do you think we'll have to ride in order to get to our part of the river?" said Phoebe.

"No time at all." Mr. Long smiled thinly. "Ms. Nettles is letting our group use the magical map so that we do not waste time."

"The map! Awesome!" breathed Phoebe.

The magical map was a perfect model of Unicorn Island. It stood in the center of the hall and could take you anywhere on the island. All you had to do was touch your hand to where you wanted to go and the map would transport you there. Students were only allowed to use it with permission.

"Go get your unicorns, then meet me and Ms. Tulip beside the map," Mr. Long instructed.

They raced to the stables to collect their unicorns. Moonbeam hardly said a word as they rode back to the school. She was obviously still upset from the previous day. Zara felt terrible. She hoped being on the camping trip would change things.

At last the girls and their unicorns arrived in the hall, weighed down by their camping gear. All the other students and teachers had left for their part of the river. There was just Ms. Tulip and Mr. Long waiting by the map. Ms. Tulip was on her unicorn, Rocket, and Mr. Long was sitting behind her, holding on tightly.

"I think Mr. Long still needs some more riding lessons," whispered Lily with a grin.

Zara giggled. Mr. Long did look very wobbly.

"Toes up!" said Ms. Tulip sternly, pointing to his feet.

Zara hid her grin.

"Gather around and hold hands, everyone," said Ms. Tulip, riding Rocket closer to the map.

"Isn't it beautiful?" whispered Phoebe, gazing at the miniature island.

"It is," answered Zara as she took her hand. "But look at how much damage the heat wave has caused." There were tiny palm trees along the coast, but the rest of the island looked hot and dry. The streams and rivers had nearly disappeared.

"Ready for the Rushing River?" Ms. Tulip touched a long, thin river that snaked through the dry landscape.

Zara gasped as the world started to spin and a wind blew up around them. Suddenly they were tumbling through the air.

Moonbeam's hooves touched solid ground, and Zara blinked in the bright sunlight.

They were standing on the bank of an exposed river that was cracked and dusty. A thin stream of water flowed slowly down the middle of what should have been a wide, fast river. Zara looked around and saw that her friends and their unicorns had arrived safely. Mr. Long was hanging on to Rocket's side, his face pale. Looking embarrassed, he quickly sat up and fixed his tie.

Ms. Tulip opened up her hand to show a small model of the academy. "This will allow us to return to the academy whenever we want," she said with a smile. "I'll put it in my tent to keep it safe until we finish."

Beyond the riverbed, there were some dry, spindly trees. The unicorns trotted over to the shade, with Moonbeam trailing dreamily behind. The girls and teachers pitched their tents next to them.

Mr. Long called for everyone to gather around. "We need to start collecting soil samples from the riverbed. Each sample you take should be put into a test tube and labeled with its exact location. You may work in pairs. Now off you go!"

They collected their equipment from Ms. Tulip and walked along the dried-up riverbed. The work took a long time. By midday, everyone was hot, sticky, and tired.

"Lunch!" called Ms. Tulip, appearing from her tent with cold juice.

"Thank goodness." Phoebe flapped her sun hat in front of her face to cool herself down. "I think I'm going to die of thirst."

While they ate their lunch, Ms. Tulip talked

to the girls while Mr. Long sat slightly off to one side.

"I'm looking forward to this evening when it'll be cooler," Aisha said to Ms. Tulip. "Can we light a fire and toast marshmallows?"

Mr. Long sniffed with disapproval. "You will not. It's far too dangerous to start a fire in these conditions."

"This trip isn't going to be any fun at all," Phoebe grumbled quietly to Zara.

"I think I'll take a walk before we get started again. Does anyone want to join me?" said Ms. Tulip.

"I'll come." Mr. Long was on his feet right away.

"Anyone else?" Ms. Tulip asked, and Mr. Long looked relieved when everyone shook their heads.

"We won't be long," Ms. Tulip said as the pair set off.

Zara watched them walk along the riverbank, and once they were out of sight, she jumped up. "This is our chance to investigate Mr. Long! Someone keep a lookout while I search his tent!"

CHAPTER 8

"Is this a good idea?" Lily asked anxiously as Zara ran to Mr. Long's tent and lifted the entrance flap. "What if he catches us?"

"I'll keep watch. If he comes back unexpectedly, then I'll pretend to have heatstroke!" said Phoebe.

"I'll help Zara search. Lily, you keep a lookout with Phoebe," said Aisha.

Zara ducked into Mr. Long's tent. It was very neat and tidy. A pair of checked pajamas was folded neatly on top of his sleeping bag.

"These are identical to my grandad's," giggled Aisha. "He's got a teddy bear!" she added. She

showed Zara a small bear covered with pink hearts. "Look at this!"

"Hang on. I've found something!" Zara held up a thin green book from Mr. Long's backpack. She paused. Someone had mentioned a green book recently, but who was it? She opened it. It was filled with notes and diagrams. She squeaked as she read a heading:

How to Cause Purple Tornadoes.

Heart racing, she carried the book outside. Why did Mr. Long have a book with notes on how to cause purple tornadoes? There was only one possible reason!

Moonbeam whinnied in surprise. "Zara! I know

that book! I've seen it in my visions. Was it in Mr. Long's tent?"

"Yes," said Zara. "Are you sure it's the one you saw in your vision, though?"

Moonbeam nodded hard. "Open it and you'll find a brown ring on the inside cover. It will look like it was made by a coffee cup."

Zara turned the book in her hands. The cover was ripped, so she couldn't read the title. Opening it up, she saw a brown stain the same size as the cup Moonbeam had described. She gasped. How was that possible?

"I told you I saw it," said Moonbeam softly, nudging her with her nose.

"Wow! You really saw it in a vision? That's amazing, Moonbeam!" said Phoebe.

Moonbeam nodded. "I . . . I think I might be a seer. It's a kind of magic that allows visions of the future."

"You found your magic?" said Lily. "I can't believe you didn't tell us!"

Moonbeam looked uncertain. "I don't know for sure yet. Zara doesn't think it is."

Zara bit her lip as her friends all gave her surprised looks. "We'll talk about this later," she said quickly. Hurt flashed across Moonbeam's eyes. "I'm sorry, Moonbeam, but for now we need to focus on this book. It's proof that Mr. Long caused all the environment problems." She held it up. "It has notes on how to cause a purple tornado and also"—she flicked the pages over—"how to cause a volcano to erupt and how to direct a tidal wave. This is the proof we need!"

"I knew it!" cried Phoebe. "Now we can tell everyone what an evil villain he is!"

"Are you sure it is Mr. Long's writing?" Aisha asked.

"I don't know," said Zara, suddenly realizing she hadn't thought about that.

"It has to be his book if it was in his tent," argued Lily.

"It seems likely, but Aisha's right—how do we know for sure he made these notes?" said Zara. She turned a few more pages. "Hey, have any of you heard of sun pearls?" she said, seeing a page entitled: *How to Cause a Drought with Sun Pearls.* They shook their heads.

Zara read the page. "It says here that while rain seeds can be used to make it rain, sun pearls can be used to cause a drought."

She read the notes out loud: *"Once the sun pearls are safe in a place where the sun will shine on them all day, the drought spreads rapidly. The spell can only be stopped by finding the sun pearls, putting them in a dried-up water source, and asking a unicorn to shed a tear on them.*" She turned the page over, but it was blank. "Maybe Mr. Long is using sun pearls to cause this drought!"

"And if we find the sun pearls he used, we can stop it!" said Lily in excitement.

"But how do we find them?" said Aisha. "They could be anywhere!"

Moonbeam stepped forward. "Maybe my magic can help?" she said shyly. "I could try to have a vision about them—it might give us some clue as to where they are."

"Go on—try!" urged Phoebe.

"I don't know if it will work," warned Moonbeam. "Visions usually just come to me. I've never *tried* to have one. But I'll give it a shot."

Zara burned with embarrassment as Moonbeam took a few steps away from them and closed her eyes. If this failed, Moonbeam was going to look so silly.

Lily squeezed Zara's arm. "It's okay," she whispered. "Even if it doesn't work, it's worth trying. Go tell Moonbeam you believe in her. It'll make her magic stronger."

Zara reminded herself about the stain inside the book. There was no way Moonbeam could have known about that unless her visions were real. *Maybe I was wrong,* she thought.

She walked over to Moonbeam and put her arms around her neck. "You can do this, Moonbeam," she said. "You *can* see into the future. I believe you." Moonbeam gave her a happy look and then shut her eyes.

For a moment nothing happened, but then she started to sway slightly. "I see a red desert," she said dreamily. "And there's a rock that looks like a bear. There's something on its nose. A shiny silver disc with some tiny white beads floating above it. They're burning hot."

"Sun pearls!" breathed Phoebe.

Moonbeam's voice rose. "I see a cloaked man now. He is angry. The earth . . . the earth is shaking. Rocks are falling from the sky. Zara!" Moonbeam's eyes snapped open. Her nostrils flared, and she was trembling. She stared at Zara with wide eyes. "I saw you in danger," she said.

Zara felt a shiver run through her, but she forced herself to stay calm. So what if Moonbeam had seen her in danger? From what she had said, it sounded like they *all* might be in danger! "Tell me about the man you saw," she said. "Was it Mr. Long?"

"He was turned away from me. I couldn't see his face," said Moonbeam. "He was tall and thin."

"Like Mr. Long," gasped Phoebe.

"We need to find the place Moonbeam saw," said Lily. "And get those sun pearls."

"If it had red soil, it might be the Ember Sands," said Zara. "There's a huge rock there called the Bear. It's very hot. It would be the perfect place to hide sun pearls."

"Should we tell Ms. Tulip?" said Aisha.

"Definitely," said Lily.

"No! Wait!" Phoebe said. "I really like Ms. Tulip, but, think about it, she's been spending a

lot of time with Mr. Long recently. What if she's working with him?"

"Ms. Tulip? No way! She'd never harm the island," said Aisha. "She's too nice."

"But what if she's just pretending!" exclaimed Phoebe. "What if she's being controlled by Mr. Long?" She shook her head. "We can't risk it. I think we should use the model to go back to school and show Ms. Nettles the book."

Zara's mind raced. Like Aisha, she found it almost impossible to believe that Ms. Tulip was evil, but could they risk it? "You're right, Phoebe," she decided. "Let's go now before Ms. Tulip and Mr. Long get back."

She ducked into Ms. Tulip's tent and took the model of the academy from the teacher's bag. The girls mounted their unicorns and linked hands. "Unicorn Academy!" they cried together.

The wind whipped up, and they found

themselves spinning around until their unicorns' hooves hit hard ground. Opening their eyes, they realized they were back in the hall of the academy.

"Let's find Ms. Nettles!" cried Zara.

The girls raced to Ms. Nettles's office. The door was open and her desk was neat and tidy, but there was no sign of her. They tried her bedroom and the stables, but the academy was empty. They ran back to the hall.

"Where is Ms. Nettles?" said Lily.

Zara glanced out the large windows, taking in the scorched grass and the shrinking lake. "I don't know, but we're running out of time. We have to try to fix the drought ourselves. Let's use the map to go to the Ember Sands, find the sun pearls, and end the heat wave. Then we can come back and find Ms. Nettles."

"But, Zara!" said Moonbeam. "In my vision, I saw you in danger in the desert. I saw the earth shaking and rocks raining down from the sky."

"It doesn't rain rocks, silly," said Zara. "That bit of your vision must have been wrong. I'll be fine." She went over and stroked Moonbeam's nose. "Moonbeam, we have to stop the drought before it's too late! Please say you'll come with me."

"Of course I'll come!" said Moonbeam. "There's no way I'll let you face danger alone."

Zara beamed. Despite their differences, she and Moonbeam were partners. They were there for each other when it mattered. "Thanks," she whispered, kissing her. Remembering what Moonbeam had said about the sun pearls being burning hot, she ran over to the fireplace and grabbed fireproof gloves. Then she vaulted onto Moonbeam's back. "Come on, everyone! It's time to travel to the Ember Sands!"

They all held hands, and Zara touched the map. A warm wind carried the girls and their unicorns to the Ember Sands. The dusty, red ground seemed to stretch on for miles. There were thorny bushes and giant balls of springy tumbleweed. The magic set the group down beside a huge rock. It was very tall, and they stepped gratefully into its shade.

Zara gazed up. The huge red rock looked just like a lumbering grizzly bear. *Bear rock!* Zara gasped. Moonbeam had said that the sun pearls were on the bear's nose, but it was impossible to see from down here. There was only one way to find out if they were actually there.

"I'll climb up to the nose," she said to the others. "It shouldn't be too bad. There are plenty of handholds and footholds."

"But—" Moonbeam began.

"No, Moonbeam, it should be me. I'm the best at climbing."

"I'll come with you," said Aisha.

"I'll be able to concentrate better if I'm on my own," said Zara. She didn't want to have to worry about someone else being in danger. She began to pull herself up its craggy face. She was a good climber, but she had never climbed so high before. She went up and up, stopping here and there to work out the best place to find a grip. Her friends' voices drifted up to her, shouting encouragement.

Zara finally reached the bear's head and stopped to catch her breath. Glancing down, she felt her stomach jump. The ground was so far away, and her friends looked so small! To her surprise, she realized that Moonbeam wasn't watching her. She was talking to Feather, who was stamping her hooves, sending pink sparks into the air. What were they doing?

Zara frowned and tore her eyes away. She couldn't afford to be distracted. Somehow, she had to edge up to the head and onto the part of rock that formed the bear's nose. She could see a strange silver disc on it. A pillar in the center of the disc was holding up a collection of round white objects. Sun pearls! Her heart lifted. Moonbeam's vision had been right. *I'll give her a huge hug when I get down and tell her I'm sorry I didn't believe her,* she thought.

She pulled herself up the bear's head and, with her feet balancing on the narrow footholds, crept across the face toward the nose. She swung herself up, her legs straddling it as if she were riding a unicorn.

The sun pearls were shining brightly, their magic coming to life in the desert sun. Zara realized that the shiny surface of the disc must be reflecting the heat back onto the pearls. It was making their magic stronger and sending it all over the

island. She could feel heat radiating from them. She would have to be careful to reach the burning pearls. She just hoped the nose would hold her weight.

She slowly crept toward the pearls. She pulled on one of the fireproof gloves and, bending forward, stretched her gloved hand out. But she couldn't quite reach the pearls over the edge of the disc. She wriggled farther, until—finally!—her fingers touched the pearls. Suddenly the rock began to shake. She heard her friends cry out and the unicorns whinny in alarm. It was an earthquake!

Forgetting about the pearls, Zara pulled her hand back and hung on to the rock for dear life. The earthquake lasted a few seconds and then stopped.

"Zara! Are you okay?" Moonbeam whinnied.

"Yes!" Zara shouted. "I've reached the pearls now. I'll be down soon. Don't worry!"

She leaned forward and, this time, her hand closed around the shining spheres. Just at that moment there was another tremor, and the rock started to shake. Zara felt herself slip and tried to hold on. But with a yell, she began to fall!

She rushed toward the ground, her arms flailing. She waited to hit the hard earth, but instead, she landed on a huge mound of springy tumbleweed. She bounced up into the air with a surprised shriek. It was like being on a giant trampoline. How had it gotten there to break her fall?

She heard her friends' voices and the unicorns' whinnies. She sat up, her hair sticking out wildly. "What just happened?" she gasped, her heart pounding.

Moonbeam cantered over. "I knew you were going to fall. I saw it in a vision as you were climbing up. So I asked Feather to use her magic to pull the tumbleweed into place."

Zara stared. "Moonbeam! Oh wow!" Shoving the pearls and glove into her pocket, she slid off the giant tumbleweed and hugged Moonbeam. "Thank you so much! You saved my life!"

There was another rumble, and the ground shook even more strongly. "I haven't finished

saving it yet!" whinnied Moonbeam as there was a loud creak from above them. "On my back! NOW!" Zara didn't stop to ask why. Trusting Moonbeam, she scrambled onto her back. Just as they leaped away, there was an enormous cracking sound and the bear's nose broke into pieces. Rocks rained down, crashing into the ground where Moonbeam and Zara had been standing.

Moonbeam skidded to a stop by the others.

"Oh my goodness, are you both okay?" Phoebe's eyes were wide with shock.

"Yes, thanks to Moonbeam," said Zara, her heart pounding like a drum. "I'll never doubt your magic again, Moonbeam. I promise!"

"No way! Look at that!" shrieked Phoebe, pointing over Zara's shoulder. "Someone's out to get us!"

Zara looked around and saw a red sandstorm

sweeping toward them, swirling viciously.

"Leave this one to me!" whinnied Shimmer.

He stamped his front hooves. Sparks flew up, and there was the sweet smell of burnt sugar. The ground seemed to ripple as a wave of energy swept from Shimmer toward the sandstorm. As it reached it, the sandstorm exploded, sending red sand shooting up into the air.

A man's voice boomed out across the desert. "You children cannot stop me! Soon everyone on this island will realize that I can do far more than unicorns can do on their own!" His cackling laughter bounced around the rock, sending chills down Zara's spine.

"We need to leave right now!" she shouted. "Moonbeam is right! This place is full of danger. The sun pearls must have been protected by dark

spells before I took them! Come on!" She pulled the model of the school out of her pocket. The others grabbed hands.

The next moment, they felt themselves being swept up in a cloud of sparkles and whisked away.

CHAPTER 10

The magic set them down safely in the hall of the academy. For a moment, they all stood there, catching their breath.

"That was the scariest thing *ever*!" said Phoebe shakily.

For once, Zara didn't tease her for being dramatic. "It really was. Oh, Moonbeam!" She leaned forward and flung her arms around Moonbeam's neck as she buried her face in her long silver mane. "Thank you so much for saving me. Seer magic is awesome."

Moonbeam turned her head to nuzzle her. "I didn't see everything. My magic only gave me glimpses. I saw visions of you and the rocks falling. I heard a man's evil laughter, and I guessed what was going to happen." Moonbeam smiled shyly at Zara. "I used the evidence. I could see that the bear's nose didn't look safe. When the earthquake started, I guessed that you would fall and the rocks would come crashing down. So I figured out how to keep you safe. I'm not going to rely just on visions in the future. I'll use evidence too."

Zara grinned. "And I'm definitely not going to rely just on evidence. If it hadn't been for your magic, Moonbeam, we wouldn't have found the sun pearls. I wish I'd listened to you sooner."

Phoebe gasped and pointed. "Your hair! Zara! You've got a silver streak—the same color as Moonbeam's mane. You've bonded!"

Zara swept her fingers through her hair, searching for the colored streak. She gasped. Phoebe was right!

The other unicorns whinnied, and the girls cheered.

"You've bonded! You've bonded!" sung Aisha.

Zara beamed. She and Moonbeam were partners for life now. They would be able to graduate together at the end of the year.

"Let's break the sun pearls' spell!" Moonbeam whinnied. "We can use Sparkle Lake."

They cantered out of the school hall and raced to the lake. The water was shrinking fast. The lake was much smaller than usual.

"Ready to break the drought?" Zara called.

"Ready!" her friends yelled back.

They walked onto the hard mud around the lake and stood in a circle. Zara pulled out the sun pearls and placed them in a little pile on the mud. They glittered brightly in the sunshine. "Unicorns, it's your turn," said Zara. "We need one of you to cry."

"I'll do it," Moonbeam said softly. She smiled at Zara and a happy tear rolled down her cheek. "I'm just so glad that you believe in me and that we've bonded." She let her tear fall onto the pyramid of sun pearls.

The sun pearls hissed as her tear fell on them, and they began to glow a bluish green. A fresh wind blew up and gray rain clouds floated across the sky. The sun disappeared behind the clouds.

"We did it!" Zara jumped up and down as the rain fell, soaking everyone and sinking into the dry ground. The girls ran to the banks and spun around, letting the rain splash onto their faces. Around them, the dry grass began to turn green, and the wilting flowers burst into bloom.

Wet but happy, the girls rode through the rain to the stables. Just as they reached the stable yard, Ms. Nettles came cantering toward them on her unicorn, Thyme.

"Amethyst dorm! Whatever are you doing back?" she said in concern. "Where are Ms. Tulip and Mr. Long?"

"We were looking for you, Ms. Nettles, but you weren't here," said Zara, ignoring her questions.

"I was at an urgent meeting with the board of trustees to discuss the extreme weather. But it looks like the drought is over," said Ms. Nettles. "Can you believe it, girls?" Her face broke into a smile, very different from her usual strict expression. "I never thought I'd be so happy to see rain!"

"We made it happen!" Phoebe said.

Ms. Nettles blinked. "You did? How?"

They all explained.

"It's got to be Mr. Long who's to blame for

everything!" Zara finished. "You have to do something about him, Ms. Nettles."

"Do you have the notebook?" Ms. Nettles said quickly.

Zara handed it over. Ms. Nettles opened it. "But this isn't Mr. Long's handwriting," she said. She looked inside the front page. "And look, here are some initials," she pointed to some faded letters. "L.T. Not E.L., which are Mr. Long's initials. He may have had the book in his tent, but it doesn't look like it belongs to him."

"He could still have used it, even if he didn't write it!" argued Zara.

"We're sure it's him, Ms. Nettles!" said Lily.

"Girls, this would be a very serious crime," said Ms. Nettles. "We can't blame anyone without proof."

"You know something?" said Aisha suddenly. "I'm not sure it is Mr. Long."

They turned to look at her in surprise.

"The voice in the sandstorm—I heard it clearly this time, and it wasn't Mr. Long's voice," said Aisha. "It was different."

"You're right," said Phoebe, frowning. She imitated the deep voice. *"You children cannot stop me!"*

Zara frowned. If the voice in the sandstorm wasn't Mr. Long's, then maybe he wasn't responsible for the weather problems after all. But why was Mr. Long acting so strangely?

"Forget about it, girls," Ms. Nettles instructed. "I will look into it. But while I do, I must ask you to keep quiet about this. Will you do that?"

They nodded.

"Good. I must use the map to go to the Rushing River and explain to Ms. Tulip and Mr. Long where you all are. They're going to be worried." Ms. Nettles straightened her glasses. "I'll make up an excuse for you having left so suddenly. I'll say Moonbeam discovered her magic, and you wanted to come tell me about a vision she'd had.

"I really am grateful to you for ending the drought. Your actions and bravery have saved the island and our dear academy. Now, it's hardly weather for camping," she said, looking at the rain, "but how would you like a special sleepover in the stables? I'll ask the chef to send you a picnic."

The girls grinned at each other. "Totally awesome!" said Phoebe. "You're the best, Ms. Nettles!"

Looking pleased, Ms. Nettles rode off toward the hall.

The girls fed the unicorns huge buckets of sky berries and dried them off. By the time they finished, the kitchen staff had laid out a huge picnic blanket covered with sandwiches, chips, and cakes. Feather used her magic to bring the camping gear they needed from the hall. The girls laid their sleeping bags around the picnic and ate.

After they had eaten, Zara jumped to her feet. "Who's up for a game of tag?"

"Me!" everyone shouted.

"You can be It, Zara!" said Phoebe. "Hide, everyone, before they tag us!" Phoebe vaulted onto Shimmer, and they galloped away to hide. The others quickly followed.

"Not fair!" said Zara, looking around at the suddenly empty space.

"Don't worry, I've got this." Moonbeam shut her eyes and swayed from side to side. "I see a girl with black hair and a unicorn with a green-silver-and-red mane galloping out from the trees in a few minutes."

"Aisha and Silver!" Zara exclaimed, hugging Moonbeam. "We can go lie in wait for them."

She grinned. "You know, something tells me we might just win this game, Moonbeam!"

"I definitely won when I got paired with you," said Moonbeam, nuzzling her.

Zara's heart swelled with happiness. "I feel exactly the same," she said. "I wouldn't want any other unicorn but you."

Zara vaulted onto Moonbeam's back. "Watch out, everyone! We're coming for you, ready or not!"

She whooped as Moonbeam galloped away, leaving a trail of silvery hoofprints on the glittering, rain-soaked grass.

Huge hailstorms are putting Unicorn Academy in danger! Can Aisha and Silver save the school before it's too late?

Read on for a peek at the next book in the Unicorn Academy Nature Magic series!

Hail battered the roof, but Aisha ignored it. She and her unicorn, Silver, were safe and warm inside the stables at Unicorn Academy. Aisha's fingers moved quickly along her flute, playing the lively piece of music she was composing for her dorm's graduation display ride. Silver tapped along with his hooves.

Aisha had almost reached the end of the piece when Lily came into Silver's stall. Aisha paused, suddenly realizing that the hailstorm had stopped and it was quiet.

"There you are! I ran over as soon as the storm ended to check that you are okay," said Lily. "The hail was huge. It did a lot of damage." Lily tucked her short dark hair behind her ears. "Trees have lost branches, and the greenhouse has been smashed." She shivered. "That's the second hailstorm in two days. It's really worrying. Zara wants us to have an Amethyst dorm meeting with our unicorns to talk about what Ms. Nettles said. Are you coming?"

Aisha remembered Ms. Nettles, the head teacher, giving a long speech that morning, but she'd been thinking about her music and had drifted off into her own thoughts. After, she'd hurried to the stables to play her piece to Silver. She frowned. "I'm working on my music."

"Please, Aisha. This is important." Lily smiled hopefully. "And we're going to play crossnet afterward. It's much more fun with four of us."

"Let's go, Aisha," pleaded Silver. "I love crossnet!"

Aisha shook her head. Her friends were great, but when she composed music, she couldn't relax until she was happy with it. It was like having an itch she had to scratch. "Sorry," she said. "You can tell me what you talked about later." She lifted her flute to her lips.

"Okay," said Lily, walking away. "But Zara won't be happy about this."

Aisha continued playing her music while Silver munched on his hay, until the stall door swung open. Aisha blinked in surprise when she saw Zara, Phoebe, and Lily all standing there. Zara's hands were on her hips. "Aisha," she said sternly. "Lily said you're too busy to come to our dorm meeting."

Behind Zara, Lily gave Aisha an apologetic look and shrugged.

"I'm working on my music," said Aisha. She put her flute down and tightened her high ponytail.

"Aren't you worried about what Ms. Nettles said?" Zara asked.

"It's awful!" exclaimed Phoebe. "Please come with us to talk about it, pleeeeeease!"

Aisha felt her lips twitch. Phoebe was always so dramatic.

"We're not leaving without you," Zara told her.

Aisha grinned. She knew when she wouldn't win. "All right," she said, putting her flute in its case. "I'll come."

"Yay!" Silver whinnied in delight. "We can play crossnet!" He eagerly trotted over to the other unicorns.

"So, what did you think about what Ms. Nettles said?" Zara asked Aisha as they followed Silver. "It's really worrying, isn't it?"

"Um . . ."

Zara frowned. "Honestly, Aisha! You didn't listen? If the hailstorms get worse, then school may have to close."

New friends. New adventures.
Find a new series . . . just for you!

ISADORA MOON
For ballerina and fairy and vampire lovers

MAGIC ON THE MAP
For adventurers

UNICORN ACADEMY
For unicorn lovers

PUPPY PIRATES
For dog lovers

PuRRmaids
For mermaid and cat lovers

BALLPARK Mysteries
For sports fans

RHCB rhcbooks.com

Collect all the books in the
Horse Diaries series!